This book belongs to:

HODDER CHILDREN'S BOOKS

First published in 2014 by Hodder Children's Books
This paperback edition published in 2016

Text © Peter Bently 2014
Illustrations © Sarah Massini 2014

The moral rights of the author and illustrator have been asserted.

A CIP catalogue record of this book is available from the British Library.

ISBN: 978 1 444 93926 2

10 9 8 7 6 5 4 3 2 1

Printed and bound in China

Hodder Children's Books
An imprint of Hachette Children's Group
Part of Hodder and Stoughton Limited
Carmelite House, 50 Victoria Embankment
London, EC4Y 0DZ

An Hachette UK Company
www.hachette.co.uk

www.hachettechildrens.co.uk

For Trudy and Tira, the mum and baby who gave me the idea – P.B.
For Alexander, sprinkled with love – S.M.

A Recipe for Bedtime

Peter Bently
& Sarah Massini

Hodder
Children's
Books

Baby, baby soft and sweet,
Almost good enough to eat!

It's night-night time so come with me,
And hear my bedtime recipe.

Take a bundle full of joy
(It can be either girl or boy).

Snuggle in your arms, like so.

Unwrap gently,

top...

...to toe.

Check those tootsies,
Can you see

the little piggy?
Wee-
wee-
wee!

Add to water (not too hot).

Stir a little.   Then a lot.

Scoop up baby. Place on mat.

Dab the drips off, pat, pat, pat.

Where's that baby?

Peek - a - BOO!

Add raspberries to tummy, too.
It should be warm and soft as silk.

Wrap once more.

And then add milk.

Put in warm place. Cover tightly.
Add some kisses. Sprinkle lightly.

Leave to settle
for the night.

Sneak out softly.
Switch off the light.

Check on baby now and then.
If required, add milk again.

It often helps the job along
If you sing a little song –

Hush-a-bye fingers, hush-a-bye toes,
Hush-a-bye lips and hush-a-bye nose.
The Dream Fairy's coming to bring you sweet dreams
Down from the moon on silvery beams.
Hush-a-bye, hush-a-bye, close your eyes tight.

Night-night, my darling.
My darling, night-night.